DISNEY

RACE TO
WITCH
MOUNTAIN

A novel based on the major motion picture

Adapted by James Ponti

Based on the Screenplay Written by Matt Lopez and Mark Bomback and Andy Fickman

Based on Characters Created by Alexander Key

Executive Producers Mario Iscovich, Ann Marie Sanderlin

Produced by Andrew Gunn

Directed by Andy Fickman

DISNEP PRESS

New York

PROLOGUE

In 1947, numerous sightings of UFOs were reported across the western United States. The most famous occurred in Roswell, New Mexico, where initial news reports claimed a UFO had actually been captured by the U.S. Air Force.

Although the Air Force denied these reports, the following year it began an ongoing investigation to study the possibility of UFOs. Known as Project Blue Book, this investigation lasted for decades and researched thousands of sightings.

When Project Blue Book was officially terminated in 1970, the government maintained that there was no evidence suggesting aliens had visited Earth.

Despite this claim, many UFO experts allege that the government continues to research alien activity to this day. Most believe the research is done at the ultra-top secret Area 51, a military installation located in the Nevada desert.

In fact, the speculation about, and focus on, Area 51 has been so intense, that there has been virtually no notice or public mention of another government facility hidden just across the Nevada border in California.

It is known as . . . Witch Mountain.

CHAPTER 1

High above the Nevada desert, a fireball blazed across the night sky, its orange-and-red flames trailing along the horizon. It did not go unnoticed. Inside NORAD—the North American Aerospace Defense Command—a group of highly trained specialists observed the fireball.

Buried deep beneath Cheyenne Mountain, Colorado, NORAD had top secret and state-of-the-art equipment designed to detect missiles launched by other countries. But this fireball had not come from another country. It had come from much, *much*, farther away. In fact, the scientists had been following its path on radar long before it even reached Earth's atmosphere.

Now they were trying to determine if it was just a random piece of space junk—such as an old satellite or a meteor—falling to earth or if it were something else.

A senior analyst named Pleasence observed the steady stream of data flashing across his computer. He coolly relayed it to the group assembled behind him. "Object of unknown origin is at ninety K and descending fast," Pleasence said.

Ninety thousand feet was just over seventeen miles above the earth's surface. At the speed it was traveling, it would only be a matter of seconds before it hit the ground.

"Zero match with anything in our database," Pleasence continued. Suddenly something else caught his attention. He paused, unsure if he should pass it along. Could he be reading the data right? "It's . . . maneuvering."

The fact that it was maneuvering meant that it was definitely *not* a meteor or satellite falling toward Earth. Something, or *someone*, was steering the object.

All eyes were on the wall of video monitors. They watched as the fireball streaked faster and faster across the sky. Then it slammed into the earth and plowed deep into the desert floor.

Standing toward the back of the room, General Lawton observed the screens. He had risen to the rank of four-star general because he knew what to do in any situation—including this one. He turned to a young man sitting at the communication center.

"Get me Henry Burke on the phone," he ordered. "Now!"

Henry Burke had a lean face with dark, secretive eyes. He rarely talked, and when he did, he revealed nothing of himself. There were only two things about him that his coworkers knew for absolute certainty: he was brilliant and he did not rest until a mission was completed.

Within seconds of receiving the call from NORAD, Burke was taking long strides down the main corridor that ran through the heart of the Witch Mountain military base. In his hands, he clutched a top secret file. Two of his team members, Matheson and Pope, were practically running just to keep up with him.

Their footsteps echoed through the corridor until they burst through a pair of doors into a hangar where a flight crew had just finished prepping three Black Hawk helicopters. A military wing commander named Carson was waiting.

"Squad and equipment locked and loaded," Carson informed Burke. "I've rerouted local law and media."

This was important. Even though the fireball had landed in a desolate part of the desert, someone may have seen it. The last thing the team needed was a small-town sheriff or an ambitious young news reporter in the way at the crash site. To control the situation, they would have to be the first ones on the scene.

Once all the evidence of the impact had been cleared away, and Burke and his team determined just what had crashed, they could tell the press whatever they wanted. A slight smile crossed Burke's face as he thought about what the cover story might be. Maybe they could say it was a research balloon, just as one of his predecessors had claimed at Roswell, New Mexico, more than sixty years earlier.

In moments, the roar of three helicopters filled the hangar and the Black Hawks lifted off from Witch Mountain. They zoomed toward the crash site, flying just above the desert's surface. At night, traveling with their lights off, they were practically invisible—which was exactly how Henry Burke liked it.

Less than an hour after the crash landing, Burke and his team were on the scene. In case there was any radiation from the ship, they wore large protective hazmat suits and helmets. The silvery suits glistened in the moonlight and made the team look like aliens from a science-fiction movie.

As they walked alongside the trench made

by the impact, the team scanned the area with high-powered flashlights. The heat caused by the crash had been so intense, some of the sand had turned into tiny shards of glass. Suddenly, Carson's flashlight reflected off something metallic buried in the sand.

Quickly, the group moved closer.

So focused on their mission, the group didn't realize . . . they were being studied as well. About thirty yards away, a girl reached up her hand and gently moved some brush out of the way so she could watch Burke and his crew at work. Next to her, a boy did the same. From their hiding place, they examined the men in the strange clothes. They were careful to be quiet, but some leaves rustled and made just enough noise for Burke to hear them.

He quickly spun around and shined his flashlight right in their direction. He scanned the area for a moment but saw nothing. Still, Burke was not one to take chances.

"Extend the perimeter," he ordered. "No one gets in. Nothing gets out."

From their hiding place, two pairs of eyes took in Burke's face and his stern expression.

It was obvious this man would not be friendly.

Suddenly, Burke signaled a soldier who set a pack of search dogs loose.

There was not a moment to spare. Under cover of darkness, the pair slipped into the desert, the search dogs barking wildly right behind them.

CHAPTER 2

Las Vegas was like no other place in the world. filled with hotels and casinos shaped like massive pyramids and fairy-tale castles, it didn't even look like a real city. That was especially true at night, when giant neon signs were turned on and filled the sky with an eerie mix of color and light that seemed otherworldly. This made Vegas the perfect location for UFO Space Expo '09. What better place to talk about life in other worlds than in a city that looked like it came from one?

Jack Bruno was definitely from this world. He made his living driving a taxi. Jack didn't want to be a cabdriver, but he was good at it. Depending on the situation, he had the ability to be either friendly or menacing—a good trait for a cabbie. If he picked up a pair of newlyweds at the airport, his warm smile and easy sense of humor instantly made them feel welcome. But if some hard partyers climbed into his backseat—and Vegas had plenty of hard partyers— Jack was big enough and strong enough to keep them from getting out of hand.

At this particular moment, Jack was shaking his head as he drove his cab down the main street, known as the Strip. Even for Las Vegas, things were pretty crazy. The sidewalks were overflowing with people who had come for the convention. Many of them were dressed like characters from their favorite science-fiction movies.

At one corner, he saw three "people" cross the road together. One was dressed as a purple alien with six tentacles and another as a silvery robot with blinking lights on his chest. The third had hair and clothes like Elvis Presley—but his skin had been painted glow-in-the-dark green.

Jack was rolling his eyes when two men dressed like storm troopers from *Star Wars* signaled him to stop. They had a hard time squeezing into the taxi because of their armor and toy laser blasters.

"Imperial 'droid," one said to Jack, trying his best to sound as menacing as possible. "Drive your Genosian Starfighter to Planet Hollywood," he commanded.

Jack sighed and started the meter. A fare was a fare. In the backseat, the "troopers" laughed and began to have a pretend battle, shooting their blasters at each other. Jack tried to ignore them, but then one of them almost hit him in the back of the head with his gun. With lightning speed, Jack ripped it out of his hand.

"Hey!" yelped the trooper, his deep and scary voice suddenly replaced by a high-pitched whine. "That's mine."

Jack pointed at a sign in the front seat that read: NO WEAPONS ALLOWED.

"It's just a toy," the passenger complained. "Lighten up."

Jack shot them a withering scowl in the rearview. They quickly decided to end their battle and didn't say another word the entire way to Planet Hollywood, where the UFO convention was head-quartered.

After he dropped them off, Jack left the Strip. He headed to the airport where he hoped he might find slightly more normal passengers. There were only so many aliens he could handle in a night.

Outside the airport's baggage claim, he was waved down by an attractive woman in her thirties. He relaxed and smiled the second he saw her. Not because she was pretty, but because she was dressed in a business suit and had no tentacles, face paint, or toy weapons.

"Where to?" he asked with a friendly smile.

"Planet Hollywood, please," she said as she got into the backseat.

Jack's good mood deflated a little. He'd been hoping to avoid another miserable trip to that hotel.

And he was a bit confused. Why was this woman heading straight into the heart of geekdom? Shrugging, he pulled away from the curb and turned on his radio. For a while, the only sound was the classic rock emanating from the speakers.

The woman was wide-eyed as she looked out the window at the Vegas lights. "This place truly is like being on another planet," she observed. "So much to do and see."

Just then, Jack was startled by a pair of aliens who staggered directly in front of his cab. They were so distracted by all the lights that they didn't even notice the traffic. Luckily, Jack was an excellent driver, and he managed to swerve right around them.

"Freaks," he muttered not so quietly as he maneuvered the cab back into the flow of traffic. "Can't wait for them to get in their spaceships and fly out of here."

A few moments later they reached Planet Hollywood, and Jack pulled the taxi up to the main entrance.

"I understand your reaction," the woman said as she pointed toward a group of ridiculously dressed convention-goers. "They certainly aren't helping our cause."

"*Our* cause?" Jack repeated. She was one of them?

"Educating the public about the possibility of life on other planets," she explained.

Jack was stunned. She *was* one of them.

"As a matter of fact," she continued, "I'm giving a lecture on astrophysical anomaly detection at the convention. Feel free to stop by. Closed-minded skeptics are always welcome."

She handed him a flyer advertising her lecture. It had all of the basic information about her talk as well as a very scholarly-looking picture of her. Underneath the picture it gave her name: Dr. Alex Friedman.

CHAPTER 3

The next morning, as the sun rose over a distant ridge, Henry Burke and his team were hard at work investigating the crash site. A cover story about a mysterious chlorine spill had done its job, and area roads were blocked off for miles in every direction. No civilians would disturb the scene of the accident. Burke was in total control.

In the early-morning sunlight, they could see much more than the night before. One group scoured the long trench where the flying object had burrowed into the ground. They took photographs and used metal detectors to make sure there were no remnants of the craft left behind in the dirt. At the far end of the trench, there was a gaping hole where the object had been pulled from the sand before being transported back to Witch Mountain.

Burke and his assistants, Pope and Matheson, were now searching the hillside where they thought they had heard something the night before. Pope, a fresh-faced scientist straight out of MIT, was just about to take a step, when Burke reached over and grabbed his leg in midair.

Pope instantly realized his mistake. He moved back so as not to disturb anything, while Burke pulled out an ultraviolet light and waved it over the ground Pope had nearly stepped on. Under the light, they were able to make out footprints. From the looks of them, they had definitely not been made by any animal native to the desert.

"Cast it," Burke instructed Matheson as he moved the light forward and illuminated several more footprints. "Cast all of them."

Fifteen minutes later, Matheson was inside the mobile command center that had been set up at the crash site. The center was sleek and modern and filled with computers, monitors, and all sorts of electronic devices.

Matheson had arranged the plaster casts he had taken along a table and was studying them with microscope goggles. Burke, Pope, and Carson all watched.

"There's a distinct pattern alternating between the depth of the impressions—a differing weight distribution," Matheson explained, "suggesting not one, but two separate EBEs." EBE stood for Extraterrestrial Biological Entity.

Burke looked down at the casts and considered what the scientist was telling him.

"They were moving fast. Bipedal," Matheson continued. He looked up at the other members of the team and took a deep breath before adding, "Possibly . . . humanoid in form."

He locked eyes with Burke. This was by far

the biggest discovery they had ever uncovered.

The moment was interrupted by Pope. As usual, he was enthusiastic, to say the least. "How awesome is that?" he asked, his voice cracking. "I mean those little nanomicrobes that were found in that Mars rock were cool, but"—he paused—"nowhere near as cool as aliens—who run!"

The three other men turned and stared at him, their expressions stern. Pope had said the *A* word. Gulping, he pretended to be fascinated by the footprint casts.

Burke instantly began instructing the others. "Review every data-gathering entity within a fifty-mile radius, starting on impact." He scanned their faces to make sure they understood exactly what they were looking for. "Hunt for the anomaly."

CHAPTER 4

While Burke was starting his hunt, Jack was getting ready to begin another shift. Quickly, he walked into the taxi garage to where a line of cabs were parked. They had been fueled up and cleaned out and were ready to hit the streets. Although a sign declared that the area was for taxis only, a large black SUV was blocking Jack's cab.

The windows of the SUV were too dark for him to see through, but he had a pretty good idea of who was in there. Once he got close, a door opened and out stepped Frank, a large man whose suit was stretched to the limit trying to cover his massive body.

"Jack," Frank said, moving toward him, "you don't return calls anymore."

Marty, another big man in a suit, stepped out from the other side of the SUV. "Mr. Wolfe thinks you're being rude," Marty said.

Their boss was not a nice man. And right now, he was rather unhappy with Jack. Whenever Mr. Wolfe was upset with someone, it was Frank and Marty's job to deliver threats and, when necessary, physical punishment. They terrified most people, but Jack could be just as intimidating. He stared Marty right in the eye.

"Tell Wolfe that when I said the last time was the last time, I meant it was the last time."

Frank let out a menacing laugh. "Mr. Wolfe decides when it's the last time. Not you, Jack."

Marty decided to try a friendlier approach. "He likes you, Jack. Hates to see you wasting your God-given talent giving fat tourists cab rides up and down the Strip. What kind of life is that?"

"One that I'm late for," Jack answered as he tried to squeeze past them to the cab's driver-side door.

Reaching out, Frank went to grab Jack. With lightning-quick speed, Jack gripped Frank by the wrist and twisted his arm behind his back. Frank let out a quick yelp of pain as Jack slam his attacker's face into the cab's hood with a loud *thud*.

Now Marty lunged at him. But Jack managed to grab Marty with his other hand and slam his attacker's face against the cab. In seconds, Jack had both thugs pinned against the hood.

"Section eight, paragraph three," Jack said, reciting from the Nevada code of taxi statutes and regulations. "As a fully licensed cabdriver in the state of Nevada, I am within my rights to deny passage to any potential fare I consider dangerous. You are, of course, entitled to file a written complaint with the state."

Satisfied that he had made his point, Jack released both men, got into his cab, and drove off. As he drove, he attempted to calm his racing heart. The traffic wasn't helping. Trying to maneuver around it, he glanced in the rearview mirror—and slammed on the brakes. Sitting in the backseat were two teenagers, a boy and a girl, who had definitely *not* been there before.

Jack stopped right there in the middle of traffic, causing a chain reaction of other cars slamming on their brakes and swerving to miss him. Jack spun around to look at his passengers.

"Where did you come from?" he demanded.

"Outside," the boy answered.

"I figured that part out on my own," Jack snapped. "How did you get into my car?"

The girl pointed at the door. "Through that portal."

Jack couldn't make any sense of this. Even after the distraction of the argument with the goons, he would have heard, or at least seen, them come through the door. Besides, he wondered, what teenager calls a door a *portal*?

Traffic was backing up, and angry drivers were honking their horns. With no other choice, Jack put the taxi into drive and started down the street.

"I am Seth," the boy said. Then he pointed to the girl. "My sister, Sara. We require your transportation services immediately," Seth continued.

Jack gave Seth a skeptical look and said, "Well, I require—"

Before he could finish, Sara completed his sentence for him. "A currency transaction."

Again with the strange slang, Jack mused.

Seth reached over the front seat to show Jack a huge wad of cash. "Will this amount suffice?" he asked.

"What did you do?" Jack asked, his eyes wide. "Rob a bank?"

"Is this acceptable, Jack Bruno?" Sara asked.

"Wait," Jack said. "How did you know my name?"

Sara pointed at the cabdriver's license, which was displayed by the meter.

"If we have a deal for your services, we must move forward rapidly," Seth insisted. "It is urgent we get to our destination without delay."

Jack hesitated. There was something *very* strange

about these kids, especially the way they talked. Then again, "strange" was a word that could have described many of Jack's customers. And their money sure was real enough. . . .

"All right, all right," Jack said. "Where to?"

Seth and Sara shared a look. They didn't know how to describe where they wanted to go. Seth reached into his pocket and pulled out a device that looked a lot like a compass.

"I need an address," Jack said. "I'm not a mind reader."

"We need to travel in *that* direction," Sara said, pointing to the highway entrance ramp.

Jack almost groaned. Already this was proving to be a troublesome fare. "Gonna need something a little more specific than 'that direction,'" he said.

Seth nodded. "We must locate latitude 40.54 cross-intersecting longitude 117.48 within a fractional percentage."

That's a real help, Jack almost said. Instead, he commented, "I think we're going to just stick with 'that direction.'"

CHAPTER 5

The mobile command center was a hotbed of activity.

As Burke's team manned superfast computers wired into a variety of government, satellite, law-enforcement, and security networks, he paced. Back and forth he strode, his eyes scanning the nonstop stream of images that zipped across the many screens.

Carson was marking locations on a computer map interface that used aerial images of the crash scene and surrounding areas. "We tracked the two sets of EBE footprints on and off for 7.3 miles," he informed Burke. "Finally losing them at a rest stop off the highway." A line on his computer screen blinked, indicating the path of the footprints. Carson clicked at the end of the trail, and security-camera images of the rest stop grew larger on the screen.

Pope, meanwhile, was rapidly searching through a database of law-enforcement logs and police-incident reports. One entry stood out. "Four hours and nineteen minutes post-impact, there was a highway-patrol incident report filed at that very same rest stop," he said excitedly.

Pope quickly typed a password override and was able to read the entire incident report.

"A car trunk burglarized," he said as he quickly scanned the patrolman's report. "No sign of forced entry. No valuables taken . . ."

Burke didn't hide his frustration. "Give me something better than that, Mr. Pope," he demanded.

Pope smiled as he continued reading from the incident report. ". . . except for clothing belonging to a fifteen-year-old-boy and girl." He turned and looked right at his boss, eager to impress him. "I think it's better than a possibility that they look human."

The group considered this development. Up to this point, all they had to go on were footprints. But this information indicated that the aliens looked like a teenage boy and girl, and that changed everything.

Carson shook his head. "They can hide in plain sight."

But Burke wasn't discouraged. He always liked a good challenge, and at least they were getting somewhere. "We're in the game, people," he told them. "Two kids don't walk down the highway alone at night. I need some options on how they were able to evade capture."

Carson's fingers started dancing across his keyboard as he scanned through video stills from a security camera at the rest stop. He slowed down when the time stamp on the video neared the time of the incident report. For a few minutes there was absolutely no activity. Then he froze the tape on an image of a tour bus.

"We have a bus landing roughly at the same time

at the same rest stop," he said. Carson shuttled through the video of passengers getting off the bus to stretch their legs or use the restroom.

"Thirty-nine people exit," he said as the last one got off. Then he sped the images forward until the people started getting back on board. "It looks like the bus picked up some extra baggage." He hit a button, and the image froze.

The black-and-white image was taken at night and was grainy, but there was no mistaking what they saw. There were now two new figures in the middle of the group, and they were getting back on the bus. They couldn't see their faces, but both appeared to be teenagers.

"We have a mode of escape and an extraction point," Burke called out to the others. "I need to know where the package was delivered. We're losing time."

Matheson didn't need to be told twice. He zoomed the camera in. "Nevada plates: Charlie-Peru-3-5-5-3-1," he read while simultaneously typing them into his computer. Within seconds a flood of information started running across his screen.

"Silver State Trailways," he continued. "Route schedule indicates . . . next stop . . . Sin City."

"Odds are strong our targets are in Las Vegas," Burke said, looming over the others. "Find them."

Pope didn't need to be told twice. He hacked into a camera feed from outside the city's main bus terminal and announced, "Eight twenty-five a.m. the vehicle rolled into the Silver State Trailways depot on Ogden Avenue."

They were getting closer. Pope scrolled through the footage until something caught his eye. As he zoomed in, the grainy image got even more difficult to see. The group still couldn't make out the faces, but it looked like the same two kids from the rest stop were in the picture.

"Our targets have entered a heavily populated city," Burke announced. "Too many unmanageable options for hiding and human interaction. I want total access to every single surveillance camera Vegas has."

Anticipating Burke's order, Carson had already

bypassed two separate firewalls and was deep inside the grid of cameras that were positioned throughout the city. "We're interlinking the system," he informed Burke.

Despite the amazing speed and skill his team was displaying, Burke was not satisfied. He wanted results. Every second lost increased the chance of these two disappearing—for good. That was unacceptable.

"The targets are on foot," he reminded everyone. "Walk with them."

In a flash, maps of Las Vegas appeared on their screens, and they started tracing out possible routes the teenagers may have used after leaving the bus station.

"We have their vehicle," Burke said, "so we know they didn't fly away. They're out there somewhere."

"Freeman Street at Main to be exact," Matheson informed the others. "I have activity at an ATM. Twelve forty-three p.m."

Once again, he brought up a grainy image taken by a security camera. On the video, two teenagers carefully approached the automated teller machine. They didn't come all the way up to it, though, so their faces were still off-camera. As the men watched, suddenly, even though neither kid had moved even a finger, the ATM started spitting out a steady stream of cash.

"Bank records indicate they withdrew the entire contents of the machine," he continued. "They never used a card, and they never touched the machine. Not once."

"Whoa," Pope gasped. This was the real deal. "Nice trick."

Burke considered the video and what it meant. "Gentlemen, it seems our EBEs possess some extraordinary skills."

Carson's eyes lit up as something else on the video feed caught his eye. "Who found themselves a ride? Stewart Avenue, one twenty-nine p.m. Keep your eyes on the yellow cab, lower left of the screen."

As they looked at the monitor, they saw the two teenagers approaching Jack's cab. Right before getting in, they turned back toward the camera. For the first time Burke and his team got a glimpse of Seth's and Sara's faces. The image remained frozen on the screen.

Burke studied their faces on the monitor, trying to take a mental picture. Even though the black-and-white footage was hard to make out, their eyes were haunting.

What were they hiding? And more importantly, why were they here?

CHAPTER 6

As Jack's cab drove along the highway far north of Las Vegas, he wondered—not for the first time—if taking this fare had been a mistake. He looked over his shoulder at Seth and Sara.

"Are we there yet?" he asked. The subtle joke was lost on the kids.

"We are not there yet, Jack Bruno," Sara said. She rubbed a pendant that hung around her neck.

The meter was already at $397.85 and climbing fast. "Your parents going to be okay with spending all this money?" he asked.

"We have previously agreed upon our financial deal," Seth said, his tone, as usual, serious. "If your concern is . . ."

Jack cut him off before he could finish. "My concern is that I got two kids with a wad of cash and a drop-off location in the middle of nowhere," he responded. "Which in my book reads like a chapter called 'Running Away.'"

"Jack Bruno," Sara interrupted. "Those vehicles behind us are indicating a pattern of pursuit."

"As a counter maneuver," Seth added, "I would suggest you increase your velocity to maximum thrust."

"Speeding? Not on your life. Speeding gets you tickets and tickets cost money," Jack said as he looked at a stack of unpaid parking tickets on the passenger seat. "And if you don't pay them off and you get one more ticket, you lose your license." He looked over his shoulder at them. "Jack Bruno *can't* lose his license." He looked through the rear window and didn't see any cars on the road.

"Besides," he added, "there are no vehicles behind us."

Just then a large black SUV came into view behind him. Suddenly two more SUVs appeared behind the first one.

"At your current rate of speed versus theirs," Seth quickly computed, "they will overtake our vehicle in less than one mile."

Jack shook his head. "Just because they're speeding, doesn't mean they're following us," he assured them. "People speed."

Even though Jack had said it, he wasn't exactly sure he was right. He checked the rearview mirror and saw that the cars *were* gaining fast.

"I'm going to let them pass," he said.

Jack slowed down to forty-five miles per hour, expecting them to zip right by. Instead, the SUVs slowed down to match his speed.

That was a little suspect. Still, he'd rather give them the benefit of the doubt. Jack rolled down his window and waved for them to pass. "Open road, people," he called out. "It's all yours."

He checked his side mirror, but they gave no indication of trying to pass. Definitely suspect. Squinting, he tried to get a glimpse of who was in the vehicle, but the windows were too tinted.

The lead SUV started to pull up right alongside Jack's cab. First it pulled up even with the backseat, so it seemed to Jack that whoever was inside could take a long look at Seth and Sara. Then it pulled up to the front seat so that they could look at Jack, too.

Suddenly, the lead SUV pulled ahead and passed the cab. Jack breathed a sigh of relief and looked back at the kids.

"See, what did I tell you?"

But he had spoken too soon.

"Jack Bruno!" Sara yelled from the backseat as she pointed toward the windshield.

Jack whipped around and saw the SUV perform a tricky maneuver that spun it around and had it coming to a stop directly in front of them.

As Jack slammed on the brakes, another SUV purposely slammed into the back of their car.

With amazing speed, Jack yanked on the

emergency brake, causing the car to fishtail. Then he gunned the accelerator so that it spun back around. It was an expert maneuver that allowed the taxi to miss both vehicles. Clearly, Jack had more than just cab-driving experience.

"Get down!" he ordered Sara and Seth. "Both of you! Now!"

The SUVs kept chasing Jack, trying to squeeze him in.

"Hold on!" he warned the kids just before he slammed on the brakes again. When he did, the two SUVs that were about to push into the cab shot past them and slammed into each other instead. They spun out of control and flipped over onto the side of the highway.

Once those two SUVs were out of the picture, Jack gunned the gas again and roared past them down the highway. There was only one vehicle left chasing him.

Jack assumed that these were more of Wolfe's goons trying to send him a message. But they weren't. It was Burke's team.

Sitting in the remaining SUV, Burke was re-evaluating the man they were pursuing. He had just taken out two specially trained military pursuit drivers.

"He *is* just a cabdriver, correct?" Burke asked.

Carson was at the wheel. He shifted into high gear to stay on Jack's tail, his eyes shooting daggers.

Meanwhile, in the backseat of the cab, Seth was taking matters into his own hands. He pulled his knees up to his chest as if he were making a cannonball and squinted in concentration. Unbeknownst to Jack, Seth's body started to dematerialize! He phased through the backseat and right through the cab itself.

He rematerialized on the side of the highway. Purposefully, he strode into the middle of the road—directly in the path of the oncoming vehicle!

"Look out!" Burke yelled from inside the SUV.

Carson slammed on the brakes, but it was too late. The vehicle crashed into Seth. But instead of hurting the boy, the SUV catapulted into the air, did a complete roll, and skidded along the highway. It came to a stop, a tangled mass of metal.

Inside the cab, Sara panicked. She was not about to leave her brother behind. Using her own tele-kinetic powers, she mentally took control of Jack's taxi. First she made the brakes lock, causing the car to skid to a stop.

"What now?" Jack asked, confused.

Then the tires started spinning backward, and the cab raced down the highway in reverse. Jack pumped the brakes, but the cab's speed kept increasing.

Back at the wreckage of Burke's SUV, Seth phased right through the tangled metal until he was hovering face-to-face with Burke.

The two stared at each other for a moment before Seth gave a warning: "Stop following us!"

Burke was too stunned to react. Seth phased back through the wreckage and onto the road. Burke looked up and saw Jack's cab heading right for them.

"Get out! Get out!" he yelled to the others in the SUV, but there was no time. The four of them braced for impact. But the taxi miraculously came to a stop—inches away from them.

Jack took a deep breath. "You both okay?" he asked, clutching the steering wheel.

"We are," Sara said.

Just then Seth phased back into the cab. Jack had no idea that he'd been gone.

"We should just keep moving," Seth said.

Jack didn't need to be told twice. If those men were connected to Wolfe, he wanted to be as far from them as possible. He hit the gas and sped away.

Burke watched as the taxi disappeared into the horizon. "I want a complete profile on the driver," he told his team.

Matheson nodded. "Do you think he's collaborating?"

Burke wasn't sure how much Jack knew about the passengers in the back of his cab. But as far as he was concerned, it didn't matter.

"Either way, he's a liability," he answered.

CHAPTER 7

As evening became night and the sun rested on the horizon, the desert was at its most beautiful and peaceful. Jack wasn't so concerned with the beauty, but he certainly appreciated the peace. It was a welcome change after the game of demolition derby that had just been played out on the highway.

"We're here, Jack Bruno," Sara said, breaking into Jack's thoughts.

Jack eased his foot off the accelerator and looked around. He didn't see anything but desert.

"Here?" he asked, puzzled. "There's nothing here."

Sara motioned ahead of them, and Jack noticed a small dirt road about twenty yards away.

"Go figure," he said, somewhat surprised. "You really do know your way." He turned, and the cab rattled and bounced along the dirt road for about half a mile. Finally, they reached a dark, deserted cabin.

"There's someone expecting you two, right?" Jack asked as he warily eyed the building. "'Cause it doesn't look like they're home."

The sun had completely set, and long shadows dominated the landscape. The beautiful desert had suddenly turned ominous and threatening.

"Do not worry, Jack Bruno," Sara reassured him. "We will soon be reunited with relatives."

Jack put the car in park and turned to the kids.

"All right, the fare comes to $721.80," he told them. "But after everything that went down today, how about I knock twenty-five percent off?"

In response, Seth shoved all of his money into Jack's hand. Neither of the kids said a word as they hurried out of the cab and toward the cabin.

"Okay, then, good-bye to you, too," Jack said to himself. It was only fitting that the strangest fare of his life had ended in a decidedly unusual way.

Looking at his reflection in the rearview mirror, he thought back on the day. He was totally exhausted.

"I've got to get another job," he told himself.

Sighing, he looked down at the money and began to count it. "I got a fifteen-thousand-dollar tip," he said when he had finished counting. "That seems *reasonable*."

Part of Jack just wanted to take the money and race back to Vegas. But he knew that wasn't *reasonable*. None of this was reasonable. And, for some reason, he felt that he needed to look after Seth and Sara. He got out of the taxi and headed to the cabin, determined to do the right thing.

"Hey, you guys overpaid . . . by a lot," he called out. He looked around, but there was no sign of Seth or Sara. It was as if they had vanished into the night. Just then he heard the sound of glass shattering.

"Hello," he called out, a little louder this time. "Everything okay in there?"

The closer he got to the cabin, the scarier it seemed. It was very dark, and most of the windows were boarded up. He looked at the porch and saw the cause of the noise. Broken glass lay on the wooden planks. Something was strange about it. It looked as if someone had broken the window from the *inside*.

Jack wasn't easily scared. But nevertheless, he was cautious as he entered. The door was partially open, and he was able to slip in without making a sound.

The inside of the cabin was spookier than the outside. A light fixture hung from the ceiling and swung back and forth, sweeping the room with a solitary shaft of light.

With each swing, Jack could make out a little more detail in the ransacked room. Furniture was tipped over in every direction, and there were broken plates and glasses scattered across the floor.

Jack heard something moving ahead of him, but before he could check it out someone grabbed his jacket and pulled him to the floor. Jack picked up a long piece of wood and swung . . . right through Seth. Jack brought his arm down and stared at Seth. He and Sara were hiding behind a couch.

"What's going—" Jack began to ask.

Seth signaled him to be quiet and started to fiddle with his compass.

"Jack Bruno," Sara whispered, "you should not have jeopardized your life by following us."

Seth's compass was now emitting a series of lights and beeps.

"What sort of trouble are you two in?" Jack asked in a hushed whisper.

"This is neither your concern nor battle," Seth said.

"Seth," Sara observed, "he's just trying to help."

But Seth didn't want to hear it. Just then, his compass seemed to lock on a heading. He signaled for Sara to follow him into the next room.

Jack was so focused on the kids, he didn't notice that when the light swung by, it momentarily illuminated another figure in the room. This figure wore a frightening mask and black armor. What Jack didn't know was that it was a Siphon—an alien assassin.

As suddenly as he had arrived, the Siphon disappeared. He was not interested in Jack. He wanted Seth and Sara.

Oblivious to the threat, Jack watched as Seth snuck up to an old refrigerator and opened it. Seth attached the compass to the back of the refrigerator. It suddenly lit up and spun into action, first one way and then another, like the dial on a high-tech safe.

Suddenly, the back of the refrigerator opened to reveal a secret passageway. Seth and Sara quickly disappeared through the door.

Jack couldn't believe what he was seeing. "Don't go in the pimped-out fridge," he told himself as he took a deep breath. But he knew he had no choice. He had to follow them. He couldn't just leave the kids alone, but there was no way he would go unarmed. Grabbing a fireplace poker, he walked into the fridge.

The door led to a stone staircase which in turn went down into a lush, beautiful underground garden. There were large multicolored orbs that pulsed with swirling gases among the plants and trees.

"What exactly *is* this place?" Jack asked as he looked around in astonishment.

Seth and Sara did not respond. They had followed the compass to a large glowing orb. Sara slipped the pendant off her neck and slid it into the orb like a key into a lock. Amazingly, the object opened to reveal a small device. For the first time since he had met them, Jack saw both Sara and Seth smile.

"What is it?" Jack asked.

"It is what we came for, Jack Bruno," Sara told him.

Jack raised an eyebrow. "Really?" he asked. "Would anyone else be looking for it . . . like, say the person who trashed upstairs?"

Seth answered. "It is very valuable," he said matter–of–factly.

Suddenly, they were startled by a noise from

above. Someone else was coming through the secret passageway!

Jack tightened his grip on the poker. Beside him, Sara removed the device from the glowing orb. As quietly as possible, they moved into the dense foliage of the garden and waited.

They could not see the intruder, but they *could* see the rustling of leaves and swaying of trees as whatever it was moved through the garden looking for them. It was the Siphon!

His heart racing, Jack tried to figure out a plan. If they made a run for it, they'd give away their position and might not be able to make it to the stairway in time. But they couldn't just wait. The Siphon was getting closer.

"Run!" Jack cried.

As Seth and Sara leaped out of the foliage, the Siphon's eyes locked on them. The chase was on!

Sara and Seth sprinted for the passageway, but there was no way they'd be able to outrun the Siphon. It quickly charged to cut them off. Just as the Siphon was about to reach them, Jack popped out from behind the bushes and smashed the creature on the head with the poker.

Much to Jack's amazement, the rod did virtually no damage. But the backhand slap the Siphon gave him *did* do damage to Jack. He went flying backward and landed with a *thud* on the hard ground. Rolling over, Jack took refuge in the foliage.

Not to be distracted, the Siphon held out his arm, and a gun materialized from his armor. He fired . . . right into one of the gas orbs! The blast struck true, causing the orb to explode in a burst of fire. This set off a chain reaction of explosions and fireballs. In a matter of seconds, the garden was engulfed in flames.

Jumping to his feet, Jack scanned the garden. He didn't see Seth or Sara . . . or the invader. Suddenly, his eyes landed on the kids. They were surrounded by a ring of fire!

As fast as he could, Jack raced to them. But just then, the Siphon burst from the flames and grabbed the device from Sara's hand. She screamed. Turning, Seth saw what had happened and attacked the

Siphon. With the attacker distracted, Sara was able to snatch back the device. Then she used her powers to uproot a burning tree and slam it into the Siphon's body.

It knocked the invader off balance long enough for the trio to hurry toward the stairs. But just as they reached them, Seth looked back and saw that the Siphon was firing his weapon—a sonic cannon that sent out a massive shock wave. Jack could see the air ripple as the concussive energy came closer and closer.

"We gotta move!" Jack yelled.

But Seth had turned and begun to dematerialize and expand his body so that it formed a shield to protect his sister. He absorbed most of the energy from the shock wave, but it still knocked the others to the ground and sent an earthquakelike tremor through the entire garden.

"Seth!" Sara cried out as his body fell to the now-crumbling steps.

Jack picked up Seth and ran upstairs. They burst through the passageway into the cabin, which was now filled with fire and smoke. Jack kept running, Seth in his arms and Sara right behind him. He kicked out the door, and they raced to the taxi just as the burning cabin started to collapse into a hole in the earth.

CHAPTER 8

With the fire climbing high into the night sky behind it, Jack's taxi hurtled down the dirt road and onto the highway.

"How's your brother doing?" he asked Sara once he'd caught his breath.

"I will be fine," Seth answered for her. "It is important that we gain much distance from this location."

"Glad you're feeling better," Jack said, trying to stay calm. The adrenaline was no longer pumping through his veins. He now felt mainly disbelief, not to mention quite a bit of anger. "You'll need your strength to explain to me . . . WHAT JUST HAPPENED BACK THERE!?"

Jack waited for a response, but there was only silence.

"Feel free to just dive on in," he continued. "We can start with whose cabin it was. Or what was growing underground?"

He paused. "Or, hey, I got a fun one. Maybe you could tell me who the guy in the robot suit trying to kill us was?"

Sara and Seth remained silent.

Jack had had enough. Slamming on the brakes, he brought the taxi to a screeching halt. He spun around.

"Here's the deal," he informed them. "The cab doesn't move until your mouths do. Start talking."

"The information you are seeking is not within your grasp of understanding," Seth said.

Jack felt as if he were about to explode. "I saved your life, and now you're calling me stupid?"

"My brother means no disrespect, Jack Bruno," Sara said gently. "But we are dealing with issues outside the realm of . . . your world."

"I'm a cabdriver," he shot back. "I've had plenty of worldly . . ." His words trailed off as he saw some rather *un*earthly lights rising from the smoke. ". . . Experiences . . ."

Sara and Seth looked out the back window and saw the lights, too.

"Jack Bruno, I suggest you drive now," Sara pleaded.

"What is that?" Jack asked, transfixed by the lights.

"Just drive!" Seth yelled.

As the lights drew closer, Jack was still trying to figure out what they were. Maybe they were coming from a small airplane. But why would a plane be coming so close?

Seth turned to his sister. "Sara, we have to go."

Sara concentrated her energy on the gas pedal, and the cab started speeding forward.

"Hey!" Jack yelled as he was thrown back against his seat.

But the taxi just kept increasing speed. Jack tried to gain control of the vehicle and outrun the lights, which now seemed to be in full pursuit of them.

And they were. The lights were coming from a small spaceship piloted by the Siphon. He had escaped the fiery inferno and would not stop until he caught his target.

"What is it?" Jack yelled as the Siphon fired off a sonic blast.

A huge chunk of asphalt exploded right in front of the cab. Jack had regained full control of the cab and jerked the wheel to avoid the explosion. But as a result, the cab careened down a steep incline.

The taxi raced down the hill. It didn't help that a fog bank had rolled in, making it nearly impossible to see where they were going.

Looking through the rear window, Sara saw the lights casting an eerie glow in the fog.

"He's coming!" she warned them.

They reached the bottom of the hill, and jumped onto some train tracks. A few minutes later they raced headlong into a dark tunnel.

Cutting the lights, Jack slowed the taxi to a crawl. Maybe they would be safe in here. . . .

"We can't let him destroy it," Seth said to Sara. She was clutching the device they had retrieved from the garden.

"Who is he?" Jack demanded. "And this time I need real answers."

"A Siphon," Sara told him.

"A what?"

"He's an assassin," Seth answered. "Trained to pursue his target until his mission is completed."

"And his mission is . . . ?" Jack wanted to know.

"Us," Sara responded in a serious whisper.

Just then, the tunnel filled with light. The Siphon was back! They waited. Was this the end? Then, just when it seemed they were doomed, the lights zipped back out of the tunnel and into the night sky.

Jack let out a sigh of relief. But he didn't for a moment think they were out of danger. "We can't just sit here," he said. Cautiously, he began to drive the cab out of the tunnel. Safely outside, Jack was about to gun the engine when he noticed that the tracks ran along a cliff. On the other side was nothing but a nasty drop-off. Ahead was an iron bridge over a river.

He had barely registered the situation when a sonic blast ripped through the air. The Siphon had returned! For one terrifying moment, the taxi—and Jack, Seth, and Sara—were airborne. Then, the taxi bounced off one of the iron girders on the bridge and somehow ended up back on the tracks. But the Siphon followed them, hitting the bridge with blast after blast.

Jack clutched the wheel. His only hope was to get into the tunnel at the far end of the bridge. He pushed the pedal to the metal and with moments to spare, they entered the safety of the tunnel. There was no way an airplane could follow them, Jack thought.

But he was wrong.

The Siphon flew into the tunnel in hot pursuit.

Jack gunned the engine again and started to pull away from the Siphon. The Siphon's vehicle barely fit in the tunnel and couldn't maneuver well. Sparks shot off when the edges struck the tunnel's rocky walls.

"We can do this! We can do this!" Jack yelled to himself—and his cab—in encouragement. Just then he heard the whistle of an approaching train.

"Oh, come on!" Jack wailed. Was he never going to catch a break?

They were trapped, the Siphon pushing them from behind and a freight train coming at them from in front. Jack was driving as fast as the taxi would go, but it didn't seem possible for them to reach the end of the tunnel before the train blocked them off.

Inside the locomotive, the engineer was startled to see the two sets of lights approaching. He yanked on the brakes and blasted the horn. The train's wheels locked up and sent a shower of sparks flying in every direction.

"Faster!" Seth screamed.

"It won't go any faster," Jack yelled, his foot pressed all the way down to the floorboard.

Sara focused her concentration on the engine, giving it an extra burst of energy. The taxi rocketed out of the tunnel inches from the hurtling train.

The instant they were clear, Jack wrenched the wheel hard to the right. They slid off the tracks and down an embankment.

Behind them, the train slammed into the Siphon's spacecraft, producing a giant fireball that exploded throughout the tunnel.

CHAPTER 9

Inside a mobile command center, Henry Burke stared intently at a photo on the monitor in front of him. It was a police mug shot of Jack, taken two years earlier. Beside Burke, Pope and Matheson read Jack's file.

"Jack Bruno," Matheson said, motioning at the photo. "In and out of juvie and state pens since he was a kid." He clicked a button on his remote, and a quick series of photos of Jack skimmed across the screen.

"Grew up poor in Midland, Texas," he continued. "Showed promise driving demolition derby and dirt tracks. Ironically, at sixteen, his parents died in a car wreck." A handful of newspaper clippings appeared on the screen. A couple had pictures of Jack as a young driver. Others detailed the automobile accident that killed his parents.

Pope picked up the commentary about Jack. "Seventeen, ran away from his foster home. Came to Vegas with hopes of going from stock car to NASCAR. Instead, he found work as a wheelman for Allen Wolfe, Vegas crime boss."

Burke nodded. As the wheelman, Jack would have driven the getaway car for Wolfe and his crew. That explained why he did so well driving on the highway.

"Last bust, two years ago, grand theft auto," Pope continued. "Got out and went legit. He's been driving a cab ever since."

As Pope finished, Carson hurried into the room. "I just spoke to Dominick Firenze, dispatch at Yellow Cab Taxi," he informed them. "Bruno took a fare a significant distance out of the city. Dispatcher claims that he's been unable to make radio contact for several hours."

"Does the cab have a tracking device?" Burke asked hopefully.

Carson nodded. "Until it stopped transmitting twenty-eight minutes ago. Last location was on train tracks."

Pope raised an eyebrow. "Interestingly enough, I've been monitoring a recent report of a massive explosion on some train tracks."

All eyes were on Pope.

"A freighter collided with an unidentified object."

If Burke had been a more emotional man, he would have smiled. Instead, within minutes, the four of them had climbed into a Black Hawk helicopter and were flying toward the site of the train collision.

Unaware of Burke's approach, Jack stood on the side of the road looking under the hood of his battered taxi. Almost every part of the vehicle was busted. He shook his head as he tried to imagine how he might get the vehicle up and running again. "Couple of kids, big wad of cash, what could go wrong?" he muttered.

In the backseat, Seth and Sara looked almost as bad as the cab. Sara said something under her breath, but Seth signaled her to stay quiet.

"We cannot trust him," he whispered.

"We must," Sara responded. "I can feel it."

Still grumbling, Jack got back into the car and slumped behind the wheel.

Sara leaned forward and tapped him on the shoulder. "We know you are frustrated, Jack Bruno," she began. "But we must ask you . . ."

Jack had had enough. He snapped upright and interrupted her right there. "No, no, no," he said. "No more 'Jack Bruno' this and 'Jack Bruno' that. I've been asking for answers and . . ."

Sara answered his question before he could even ask. "It's exactly what you've been thinking, Jack Bruno."

Jack flashed an exasperated look. "So now you're

going to tell me *exactly* what I've been thinking?"

Sara nodded. Reading minds was another one of her "talents." "The Siphon, that spaceship, my brother and I . . . are indeed not from your planet."

"So that's it?" Jack said, spinning around to face them. "Mystery solved. You want me to believe that you're both aliens," he said slowly.

"It is the truth," Seth replied.

"You don't look like aliens," he said slowly.

Sara flashed Seth a confused look before asking, "What does an alien look like, Jack Bruno?"

A few days of driving people back and forth to the UFO convention had given him more than a few ideas. "You know, an alien. Little green men. Antennae. Laser guns. 'Take me to your leader, Earthlings' mumbo jumbo."

"Mumbo jumbo?" Seth asked, more confused than before.

Sara seemed to understand better. "He requires some proof," she said. "He thinks we are insulting his intelligence."

"Well, yeah," Jack said. "I mean, you don't just

drop the 'alien' bomb. I have seen some weird things today, but you can't expect me to believe . . ."

Before he could continue, loose items from throughout the cab started to lift into the air. Coins, old parking tickets, and an empty coffee cup were all floating around as if they were in outer space. Jack's mouth dropped open.

"There are things floating around me, right?" he asked, worried that he was losing his mind.

Sara nodded. "I'm telekinetic," she explained. "I have the ability to move items with my mind."

"That's impossible," Jack said, disbelieving.

"It is quite possible," Sara answered. "On our planet as well as yours. You don't do it because you haven't learned to use your full brain capacity."

"Maybe I don't do it," Jack retorted, "because it's just creepy! Could you stop that?"

In an instant, everything dropped simultaneously.

Sighing, Jack turned back around. He tried the ignition and after a few coughs, the cab started. Slowly, the taxi started to rattle down the road, it—and Jack—barely keeping it together.

★ ★ ★

Back at the crash site, flames flickered in the trees alongside the train tracks. A shadowy figure arose from the wreckage of the collision. It was the Siphon. His body was charred, but somehow he had managed to survive. His leg was severely damaged and bent in an unnatural direction. He straightened it, apparently unbothered by any pain. Then a laser emerged from among the weapons on his arm. He used the laser to burn the armor and flesh around his wound and melt it all back together.

Suddenly a noise from above caught his attention. It was the sound of a helicopter's rotors. The Siphon slinked back into the shadows to keep from being spotted.

A searchlight from the helicopter moved across the scene of the collision, as Burke and his team surveyed the wreckage.

"Train engineer is banged up but alive," Carson told the rest of the team. "Last thing he saw in the tunnel was our taxi and a set of flying lights. He figured it was a small plane."

"Small plane?" Pope asked, his curiosity piqued. "You think there's a chance they have a second spacecraft?"

Matheson shook his head. "You have the ability to fly at the speed of light, yet you use a beat-up cab?"

Burke had seen enough. "Secure the site. Catalog *every* piece of debris. I want to know what's train, what's cab, and . . . what's left."

"Roger that," Carson replied. "We've set up a trace on Bruno's cell phone. He uses it, we'll be there before he can hang up."

Burke nodded, confident that the chase was nearing its end.

CHAPTER 10

Jack's taxi was running, but just barely. It sputtered down the road and past a sign reading, ENTERING STONY CREEK—EST. 1846. Once a silver-mining camp, Stony Creek looked like the kind of small town where everybody knew everybody else. Jack also hoped it was the kind of town where you could find a great mechanic at any hour of the night.

Jack managed to nurse his cab all the way to Eddie's Service Station. As they got out of the cab, he turned to the kids. "Don't say anything. Don't touch anything. And don't do anything . . . freaky," he instructed them. Then he turned and called out to see if anyone was there.

A man who looked to be in his fifties walked out from a dusty old office. This was Eddie, who owned the garage. "We're closed," he explained.

"I know," Jack responded. "It's just we've experienced some car trouble."

Eddie shrugged. "We're still closed. Better to experience some car trouble when we're open."

"I'll plan better next time," Jack said.

"Jack Bruno," Sara said, ignoring his instructions to remain quiet. "The only thing that will convince Eddie to reopen for business will be a significant sum of money."

"Do I know you from somewhere?" the mechanic asked, looking at her carefully.

Jack didn't give Sara a chance to answer. "Nope, you don't," he assured him. He pulled the money from his pocket. "We'll pay you double your rate."

Eddie was no longer concerned about how

Sara knew his name. This was now a negotiation. "Triple," he replied.

"Done," Jack said with a satisfied smile.

A few minutes later, Eddie was hard at work on the car while Jack and the kids were walking into a nearby restaurant to get something to eat. The restaurant was nice but nothing fancy. A country band was playing on the stage, and a few couples were on the dance floor. Sara and Seth were intrigued by everything they saw.

"This settlement of Stony Creek has less lights and energy than Las Vegas city," Sara observed.

"Every place on the planet has less lights and energy than Vegas," Jack observed, smiling. Then he turned to the kids, his expression growing serious. "Look I need you two not to be 'aliens' in here. Understand?"

"No. I do not," Sara answered. "How can we not be what we are?"

Jack stifled a sigh. "Just don't do any of your creepy magic floaty stuff," he explained.

As they sat down at a table, Sara looked Jack in

the eye and said, "I hope you do not act upon your thought of making a fast break out the back door and escaping Stony Creek never to look back at us again."

Jack's eyes opened wide. "How did you know that?" he asked.

"My sister also has the gift of telepathy," Seth informed him. "She can read the minds of those nearest to her."

"Tell your sister, on Earth it's rude to read people's minds." Jack gave a little finger wag for emphasis.

Jack was a bundle of nerves, especially when the local sheriff walked in and sat at a nearby table. It seemed as if everybody was staring at them—including the sheriff and his three deputies.

Seth and Sara had gone to wash their hands when Jack's cell phone rang, startling him. It was Dominick, his boss from the cab company.

"I've been trying to get you all night!" Dominick cried. "Where are you? You dump that fare yet?"

"Not quite," Jack answered. "It's complicated."

"Un-complicate it," Dominick ordered. "I want

my cab back. Spotless." Jack cringed, thinking about how far from spotless the cab actually was.

"By the way," Dominick continued, "don't have your creditors call, looking for you here."

"Creditors?" Jack had no idea what Dominick was talking about.

"You got all kinds of people trying to find you," he said. "Pay your bills on time." Then he hung up.

Jack was confused. He didn't owe anyone money. Which meant, someone was trying to find him. Was it Wolfe? Or did it have something to do with Seth and Sara?

Unknown to Jack, Burke and his team were listening in on the call and had instantly begun tracing his location. Within moments they were rushing toward Stony Creek.

When Seth and Sara returned, Jack looked at them nervously. He had made a decision and wanted to tell them what it was.

"I think it would be . . ." he started to say.

Sara finished his statement, "best for everyone if Seth and I got another ride?"

"Seriously," Jack said, more than a little creeped out that she could read his mind, "you've got to stop doing that."

The waitress brought their orders, and when she left, he went on. "I'm sorry," Jack said, sounding genuine. "But you need someone from NASA or the air force to help you. Not me."

"If you abandon us, our mission will be in jeopardy," Sara told him.

"And the chances of our survival zero," Seth added.

Silence fell as the three ate their food. Finally, Sara spoke up. "On Earth, isn't there a difference between 'can't help,' and 'won't help'?" she asked.

Jack swallowed a bite of his food. "I'm just trying to be honest here," he said. "I'm the wrong guy."

Sara reached out and put a hand on top of Jack's. "Maybe you need help, too, Jack Bruno."

Before Jack could respond, his cell phone rang again. He answered it expecting to hear Dominick complain some more. But it was a voice he didn't recognize.

"Are they safe, Jack?" the voice asked.

Jack got up from the table so that the kids couldn't overhear him and so that Sara couldn't read his mind.

"Who is this?" Jack asked when he was far enough away from them.

"Henry Burke. I work for the Department of Defense. I handle their more sensitive cases."

"What do you mean *sensitive*?"

"I suspect we both know the answer to that question," Burke answered.

Jack's protective instincts kicked in. He looked out the window, scanning for any suspicious activity.

"Look, they're just kids," Jack told him. "They don't want any trouble. Neither do I."

"Good," Burke responded. "Then we're all on the same page. *Trouble* is the last thing I want as well. But what I *do* want is your two passengers."

There was something about Burke's voice that Jack didn't trust. He looked out the window again. Five black SUVs had driven up the otherwise empty street. They began to block off the roads, closing off escape routes.

"I have had a chance to acquaint myself with your background," Burke went on. "You're a convicted felon. You've spent most of the day breaking one law after another, for what—them?"

Jack glanced back at the table where Seth and Sara remained oblivious. "What do you want me to do?" Jack asked, sighing.

"Not make a scene," Burke replied coldly. "You walked them into the restaurant. Now you can walk them out. I'll take it from there. And to show my appreciation, I'll wipe your slate clean."

A man with a cell phone to his ear got out of one of the SUVs. Burke, he figured. A dozen or so heavily armed men fanned out around the agent.

"Just walk away?" Jack asked. "No harm, no foul?

"That's right," Burked answered. "You have five minutes. And then it will all be over."

Jack looked back at the table. Seth and Sara were gone.

"Five minutes," Jack answered, not betraying the new plan he had just come up with. "See you then."

CHAPTER 11

Jack knew he didn't have much time. Quickly, he scanned the restaurant and saw Seth and Sara over by the stage.

"We're leaving now," Jack said when he reached them.

Sara looked right at Jack and read his mind. "They're here for us, aren't they?"

"Yes, they are."

Jack was desperately trying to figure out how to buy some time, when he remembered the sheriff.

He walked over to the man's table. "Excuse me," Jack said, interrupting the sheriff's meal with his deputies.

"Can I help you?" the sheriff asked.

Jack took a quick breath. "I was just wondering what your town's policy is regarding concealed firearms?"

Jack motioned over toward the door, just as Burke and his men burst in. The timing couldn't have been better. The sheriff got up and headed over toward Burke. Jack quickly led the kids in the other direction, looking for a back door.

"Can I help you boys out?" the sheriff asked once he reached Burke, who was busy scanning all the tables.

"Official government business," Burke told him. "Move aside."

The sheriff did not take kindly to being told what to do. "Officially *my* town," he told Burke. "*My* business."

Burke repressed a groan of rage. Local law enforcement was always getting in his way. Burke

Las Vegas cabdriver Jack Bruno is about to go on an adventure that is out of this world!

In the middle of the Nevada desert, military agents discover something very strange. . . .

Seth and Sara may look like average teenagers, but they have a big secret.

Henry Burke has only one mission—find the aliens
that have crashed on Earth.

Jack isn't about to leave Seth and Sara alone in the middle of nowhere

Inside a mysterious garden, Jack realizes they are being followed.

Keeping an eye out, Jack sees something approach out of the ferns.

Dr. Alex Friedman believes extraterrestrial life is out there—she just doesn't realize how close.

Dr. Harlan shares his knowledge about the mysterious Witch Mountain.

Jack and Alex check out Witch Mountain. It looks impenetrable.

Safe inside their ship, Seth and Sara figure
a way out of Witch Mountain—and toward home.

Jack and Alex know their adventures are
only just beginning.

and his men all reached inside their jackets to pull their guns, and the sheriff and his deputies did the same. In a moment, it seemed like everyone was pointing a gun at somebody.

"You're making a mistake, Sheriff," Burke said, trying to keep his temper from erupting.

"So says every criminal arrested."

While this was going on, Jack managed to lead Seth and Sara to a hidden area behind the stage. There they found a rickety ladder that led to the roof. It wasn't ideal, but it was the best chance they had to escape.

The three of them climbed up the rungs, but when they got to the top, Jack discovered the ceiling hatch was locked—from the outside. As he tried to figure out what to do, Seth reached past him. His arm disappeared through the hatch and a moment later, the small door swung open.

Noticing Jack's astonished expression, Sara explained. "My brother has the ability to control his molecular density, allowing him to phase through solid objects or withstand the greatest of impacts."

Jack swallowed. "Neat," he said, following Seth up onto the roof as Burke's men passed by below, unaware. Jack and the kids hurried along the roof toward the back of the building.

Jack was able to climb down from the roof onto the top of a trailer and then jump to the ground. He turned back and started to help Seth and Sara down when he heard the low, fierce growl of a dog.

When Jack turned, he saw the animal only a dozen or so feet away.

"Easy, boy," Jack said, trying to sound as soothing as possible. "Nice little doggy."

It didn't do the trick. The growl intensified, and the dog bared its teeth and charged. All Jack could do was cover his face and brace himself for the attack. But it never came.

When he looked up, he saw the terrifying junk-yard dog happily licking Sara's face.

"We appreciate your understanding," Sara said to the dog. Apparently, her many gifts included the ability to communicate with animals.

"It's time to go," Sara told Jack.

★ ★ ★

nside the restaurant, Burke had managed to get a high-ranking government official on the phone with the sheriff. Once the call was over, he turned to Burke and his men. "You got yourself some mighty big friends in some mighty big places."

Burke could barely contain his rage. They had wasted valuable time! "Lock down this facility," he ordered. "No one exits until my team has checked them."

Moments later, Burke and his men discovered the hatch to the roof. They climbed up just in time to see Jack drive his cab out of Eddie's garage.

Burke grabbed his walkie-talkie to alert everyone. "The taxi is on the move. I want that cab . . . and everyone in it!"

Behind the wheel, Jack watched Burke's men race out of the restaurant, their guns drawn. Some hopped into their SUVs and started them up.

"There are way too many of them to outrun," Jack said.

Sara took a deep breath. A moment later there

was a series of explosions. Jack looked back and smiled as he saw that their windows and tires were all blown out.

"Whatever you're doing," he told Sara, "keep doing it."

Burke reached the ground just as Jack and the cab were nearing. He lifted his gun and took aim. Just as he went to pull the trigger, a loud growl filled the air, and the junkyard dog leaped out from the darkness. The dog clamped its jaws tight around Burke's arm, and the agent let out an agonizing scream as he dropped his gun to the ground. His job done, the dog jumped over a fence and away from the approaching agents.

Jack wasn't going to look a gift horse—or dog— in the mouth. "Say good-bye to Stony Creek," he said and hit the gas. But something was wrong. Instead of speeding up, the cab came to a screeching halt.

"Come on, baby, not now," Jack pleaded to the cab. Then a thought occurred to him and he turned to face Sara.

"Did you do that?" he demanded.

Sara didn't answer. She just opened her door, and the dog raced up to the taxi and jumped in beside her.

"Absolutely not!" Jack exclaimed. "Junkyard does not go with us! I'm done picking up stray passengers!"

Burke's men started shooting, and Jack realized that Sara was not going to let the cab go without the dog.

"Fine!" he relented. "Junkyard goes with us!"

Sara smiled. In a flash, the taxi was racing down the road, away from the danger.

Sara looked at Jack and smiled warmly. "Thank you, Jack Bruno," she said as they drove out of Stony Creek.

"Those men," Jack said. "They were the same ones chasing us on the highway before."

"Yes," Sara said simply.

"It is vital we find their base of operation," Seth added. "You must take us to them. Immediately."

Jack couldn't believe what he was hearing. "You

want me to 'take you' to the guys who are trying to kill you? Let me explain how we do things here on Earth. People who want you dead, you avoid. That way you stay alive. Make sense?"

"No one on your planet will stay alive if we do not return to our planet," Seth responded. "And in order to return, we need our ship. And those men trying to kill us have stolen our ship. Make sense?"

Jack felt like his head was going to explode. When had things gotten so complicated?

"Where do you suggest we begin our search?" Sara asked, convinced Jack would help.

"I don't suggest *I* begin searching at all," Jack answered.

Seth scowled. "Just as I thought," he said to his sister. "We only have each other. No human is going to help us."

Jack's spine stiffened. "Easy on the human-bashing. And for the record, I wouldn't even know how to help you."

Suddenly Jack had an idea that brought a smile

to his face. Sara read his mind but didn't know what it meant.

"Who is Dr. Alex Friedman?" she asked.

Jack laughed. "Someone who might be able to help you," he said, aiming his cab toward Vegas.

And Jack was going to need all the help he could get. Because outside of the restaurant, the Siphon watched in the shadows, waiting. He did not give chase. There would be time to act soon enough.

CHAPTER 12

In Las Vegas, Dr. Alex Friedman was halfway through her presentation—and it wasn't going well. Unlike her, most of the people at the UFO convention had not come to have an educated, scientific discussion about the possibility of life on other planets. They wanted to talk about green spacemen with fuzzy antennae.

She clicked a button, and a picture of space was displayed behind her on a large screen. "This was captured by a far-imaging telescope less than forty-eight hours ago," she explained. "I want to direct your attention to this."

Using a laser pointer, she highlighted a blotch in the picture. She was obviously very excited about the blotch, but her audience could not have been more bored.

"It looks like a smudge," one person called out.

"Yes, it does. Only . . ." She clicked another picture, which looked identical to the first one on the screen. "In the next image capture," she said, pointing her laser at the same spot, "that 'smudge' is gone."

Her big announcement was met with still more blank stares.

"Was it a spaceship," someone called out hopefully. "Did they abduct you?"

The audience began to stir.

"The aliens that abducted you, were they tall ones or short ones?" someone else called out.

"Maybe the lizard people!" another audience member shouted.

Alex couldn't believe what she was hearing. "I

wasn't abducted by anyone," she said, "much less by an alien."

"How do you know?" someone asked. "Dr. Harlan's last book was all about how the aliens erase your memory with probes. Have you read it?"

Dr. Harlan was the hero of the more "eccentric" convention-goers. Alex thought that he was something of an eccentric as well. He certainly wasn't a true scientist.

"Donald Harlan's book?" she asked. "It's pure science fiction. I'm talking about science *fact*. Hard data. Do you hear yourselves? This is why the scientific community doesn't show us any respect."

"Dr. Harlan says the scientific community has been infiltrated by alien spies," an audience member offered. "So you can't trust them."

Alex had had more than enough. "That's it," she said, forcing herself not to throw her arms in the air. "I will not take any more questions dealing with alien abductions or Dr. Harlan."

Half of the audience got up and left. Shrugging, Alex pushed a strand of brown hair behind her ear and carried on. By the time she was finished, there was no one left. As she packed up, she heard a door open. She looked up to see a man and two teenagers entering. It was Jack, Seth, and Sara.

"The cattle mutilation lecture doesn't start for an hour," she said. "But grab a seat now. This place will be packed. Always is."

"We're here to see you," Jack told her.

She looked at him. The man looked familiar. She racked her brain, trying to figure out where she had seen him before.

"It's Jack Bruno," Jack said with a friendly smile. "We met earlier."

"We did?" Alex asked, still drawing a blank.

"Cab," he reminded her. "Airport to hotel. Driver." As he said "driver," he made a little motion like he was turning a steering wheel.

"The nonbeliever," she said, remembering. "What are the odds?"

"Is there a place where we could talk?" Jack asked her.

She looked around the empty ballroom and

gave him a look. "Crowds in here making you uncomfortable."

"Someplace more private?" Jack suggested.

"Look," she said, "no offense, but I'm pretty busy and . . ."

Sara read her mind and completed her sentence for her. "Feeling stressed over her thesis on Gliese 581 and Alcubierre's warp drive."

Alex was stunned. "How did you? I didn't tell anyone."

Jack smiled. "It gets better, trust me."

Intrigued, Alex followed them to an out-of-the-way exhibit on Mars that was closed. While the kids became absorbed in images of the red planet, Jack told Alex all about them.

"Are you insane?" Alex demanded when Jack was finished.

"I thought you of all people would understand and want to help," he said, shocked by her reaction.

She looked over and noticed that Seth and Sara were no longer looking at Mars. They were now looking at her laptop.

"Hey, please don't touch that," she said.

"You captured an image of our ship," Seth said as he turned the laptop to face her. The image on the screen was the one she had shown at the presentation.

"The smudge?" she said. "You're telling me you think the smudge is your spaceship?"

"We *know* it is our spaceship," Sara corrected.

Alex had been mocked enough for one day. "That's it, I'm out," she said. "Now if you'll excuse me, I'll just grab my laptop."

As she reached to take the laptop from Seth, his hand phased right through hers. Startled, she jumped back and dropped the computer. Sara used her telekinetic power to "catch" it mere inches above the floor and then float it back up to Alex, who was totally speechless.

"Oh, right," Jack said with a smile. "They can also do that stuff."

"Who are you people?"

Sara turned to Seth. "Show her."

Seth pulled the futuristic compass out of his pocket and held it up for the others to see. The device was glowing, when suddenly the glow exploded into a blinding white light and turned the room into a sort of living planetarium. Three-dimensional images of planets and stars swirled around them as if they were in the middle of a distant galaxy.

Alex gave Jack a stunned look, but he just shrugged, as if to say, what did I tell you? She turned back to the kids. "I have so many questions!" she exclaimed. "Why did you come to Earth?"

"Our planet is dying," Sara told her calmly. "Millennia of neglect has rendered our atmosphere unbreathable."

"Our parents are scientists," Seth went on, "who have studied Earth's changing climate in hopes of finding a solution for our own planet's future."

Alex and Jack looked at each other, confused. Wasn't finding a solution a good thing? Seth shook his head. The leaders of their planet thought the answer would take too long, he explained. "It would be simplest," he finished, "to abandon our dying planet and . . . occupy yours."

"Occupy?" Alex asked, suddenly concerned. "But Earth's resources can barely sustain our own world population."

Seth nodded, his expression even more serious than usual. "Hence the need for . . . elimination."

This caught Jack's attention. "Elimination? Wait! I'm helping you conquer my planet?!"

"Not us, Jack Bruno," Sara claimed. "Most people on our planet fiercely oppose the plan."

"But fear of extinction triumphed among our people," Seth continued. "Invasion plans were drawn up. Fleets readied to launch an assault against Earth."

Jack and Alex shared another look. This did not sound promising.

"But then our parents discovered a solution!" Sara cried. "An experiment at an outpost here was successful in regenerating life into all previous dying plants and trees."

Alex's eyes widened. "Which would enable the re-oxygenating of your poisoned atmosphere," she observed. "Brilliant!"

"So what's the problem?" Jack asked. He

was beginning to wish he had paid a little more attention in science class.

"Our military preferred a solution of invasion over science," Seth answered.

"Which is why we had to hurry and retrieve the experiment." Sara held up the device they had recovered from the underground garden in the desert. "All the proof that our planet can be saved, and your planet spared, is here."

Suddenly, things were starting to make sense to Jack. But he still had questions. "Where are your parents? And what about the assassin?"

"Assassin?" Alex asked in a sudden panic. "What assassin?"

"Their work required them to stay behind," Seth said, looking oddly nervous.

Sara answered the second question. "The Siphon Warrior Series Deranian 75 were created by our military," she told Alex.

"They're bred to hunt?" Alex asked, her heart racing.

"They're bred to kill," Seth corrected. "And if we

don't return to our home in time, the invasion will proceed, and one Siphon will turn into a thousand Siphons."

Alex considered all of this for a moment. "We seriously have to find your spaceship."

Alex was right. Because at that very moment, a group of black government SUVs raced through Las Vegas.

Burke and his team were closing in—fast.

CHAPTER 13

Alex was not looking forward to what she was about to do. But if Seth and Sara were going to get their ship back, there was only one person she knew who might be able to help. Unfortunately, Dr. Harlan was not someone she usually got along with.

"How well do you know this guy?" Jack asked as they hurried out of the hotel and through the parking lot. They had managed to get Harlan's assistants to bring them to where he was holed up.

"We've done a few panels and debates together

on opposite sides," she explained as she walked. "But no one knows the shadow world of UFO government conspiracies better than Harlan."

At the edge of the parking lot, they reached a Winnebago. This was Dr. Donald Harlan's home, office, and transportation. Alex knocked.

"Go away," Harlan barked from inside. "Book signing's not until 4:30."

"Harlan," Alex called, "it's Alex Friedman."

From inside, they heard grumbling. The door swung open to reveal a disheveled older man.

"Dr. Alex Friedman," he announced victoriously. "*Quelle* surprise. To what do I owe the pleasure of the world's greatest unemployed astrophysicist visiting my humble castle on wheels?"

"Please, Harlan. We need to talk to you. It's incredibly important."

Harlan let them in, and they told him just enough so that he could help. They were careful not to reveal that Seth and Sara were aliens.

"So you're saying the three of you 'witnessed' this reported UFO crash?" Harlan asked.

"That's right," Jack said.

Alex leaned forward. "We were wondering if there was any intel out there among your sources."

"I don't like liars," Harlan told them.

Jack, Alex, Seth, and Sara all grew tense. Had they been discovered?

"Thankfully," Harlan continued, "your story matches up with reports out of SETI, NORAD, and NASA."

Harlan took a seat at one of his computers.

"You're lucky kids, that you never came face-to-face with the aliens in the craft," Harlan told Seth and Sara over his shoulder. "They'll eat your flesh."

Sara looked as if she were about to laugh. "I guess we are indeed lucky kids not to have our flesh eaten." She paused. ". . . By the aliens."

Harlan continued to type, unaware of the sarcasm. "You got that right." He punched something on the keyboard, and a satellite picture of the crash scene opened on his computer screen.

"A source e-mailed me this sat-grab," he explained. "The spot's already a blur on Google

Earth. How soon after you called it in did the suits come after you?"

"Immediately," Jack answered for them. "His name was Henry."

"Burke," Harlan said with a nod. "Interesting."

Harlan typed in a quick search command, and another picture opened up on the screen. It was a grainy photo of Burke.

"Burke was a rising star in military intelligence, chief investigator in a UFO sighting near Malmstrom Air Force Base in Montana," Harlan informed them. "Two weeks after he declared the sighting 'unsubstantiated' he retired to civilian life."

"Where would they take the spaceship?" Alex asked. "51? Nellis? Vandenberg?"

Harlan shook his head. "Given the size and scope of the crash and Henry Burke's involvement, there's really only one possibility." He glanced at his two assistants who had been silent until now.

In unison they said, "Witch Mountain."

Jack gave Alex a confused look and she just shrugged. She'd never heard of it.

Harlan flipped through a stack of black-and-white photos and pulled out a fuzzy aerial picture.

"California, fifty miles across the Nevada border," Harlan told them as he handed the picture to Alex. She held it up for Jack and the others to see. "It's one of our most top secret facilities."

Harlan got up and started rifling through a messy pile of paperwork. If there was any organization to it, the others couldn't tell.

"I got a schematic around here somewhere," he continued. "But if you're thinking about visiting, don't. When I say it's fortified up the yin-yang, it's an understatement."

Amazingly, Harlan was able to find exactly what he was looking for in the pile. He handed Alex a set of old blueprints stamped TOP SECRET.

"Thank you, Harlan," she said, meaning it. "For everything."

"Whatever trouble you're in," Harlan warned them, "trust no one."

Jack nodded and they started out the door.

"Freeze!" Harlan said, causing them all to stop in midstride.

They turned, unsure of what to expect. Harlan smiled and tossed Seth and Sara each a small pin with an alien face on it that read, DR. HARLAN FAN CLUB.

"Stay in school and keep your eyes on the sky," he told them. "Remember aliens, they'll—"

"Eat your flesh," Seth finished. "How could we forget?"

As the four left to find Witch Mountain, Jack and Alex tried not to laugh.

"We'll spread the word," Seth promised him.

CHAPTER 14

With time running out, the four, set on going to Witch Mountain, raced back into the hotel. Despite the rush, Sara wanted to make sure to tell Jack and Alex something.

"Thank you, both of you," she said. "Seth and I understand that you don't have to go forward with us. Yet you choose to."

"You're welcome," Alex said with a warm smile. She turned to Jack. "Bring your cab around. I'll grab my stuff and meet you in the lobby." Next she addressed the kids. "Don't worry. We're going to get you home. I promise."

Her confidence and enthusiasm helped them relax, and they nodded. Jack tried to talk her out of coming, but there was no way she would miss it— or leave the kids stranded.

"Just lay low till I get back," Alex instructed.

"Laying low," Jack said with a nervous shrug. "How hard can that be?"

Alex rushed off to her room, and Jack turned to face the two kids, who were both smiling. He eyed them suspiciously.

"She thinks you are very handsome," Sara told him. "And potentially much smarter than you act."

"Really?" Jack said, suddenly smiling, too. After all, Sara wasn't just a gossip. "She was thinking about me?"

Jack wouldn't have been smiling if he knew that Burke and his team had arrived and were entering the main lobby, greeted by a friendly concierge. "Welcome to Planet Hollywood. Are you gentlemen here for the UFO Space Expo?"

"Wouldn't miss it," hissed Burke as his eyes started searching the crowd for aliens far more authentic than any of the convention-goers could ever have imagined in their wildest dreams.

Meanwhile, Jack's smile had faded when he noticed Seth and Sara had disappeared into the crowd. Frantically, he began searching the exhibit hall and found them watching a play. "Is this a re-enactment of a piece of Earth's important history?" Sara asked, motioning to the play in progress.

Jack looked up and saw the poor quality sets and the bad alien costumes and just shook his head. "No. This is nerdy."

Seth gave him a look. "What is *nerdy*?"

"You know nerdy," Jack said trying to think of a good description. "Like people who believe in all this alien stuff."

Seth smiled. "Like you?"

Before he could answer, something caught Sara's eye.

"Jack Bruno," she said pointing to the other side of the stage.

It was the Siphon. He was stalking his way through the crowd, his robotlike armor blending in perfectly with the costumed characters.

"Impossible," Jack said, shocked. How had that thing survived the explosion?

The Siphon climbed up on the stage to get a better look at the faces in the crowd. Everybody assumed he was just part of the play.

"Oh, no!" said one of the actors doing a bad job ad-libbing a script change on the spot. "It is the arrival of the space creature from planet Gitoffthestage! Thankfully my weapon can destroy him."

The actor pulled out a phony light saber and posed like he was going to engage the Siphon in battle. The Siphon had no idea what was going on. He used one of his real lasers to slice the toy in half.

The actor was furious. "Dude, that's not in the script. You are so fired."

Just then, the Siphon spotted what he was looking for. He locked his deadly stare on Sara, Seth, and Jack and started shooting at them.

"Look out!" Jack screamed, diving for cover.

Sara used her telekinesis to move props from the play into the path of the oncoming blasts. Assuming this was all part of the show, the crowd cheered wildly as each prop exploded in midair.

Sara looked above the stage and spied a very large, very heavy-looking lighting grid hanging from the ceiling. Refocusing her energy, she broke some of the cables free, and the entire metal structure swung down and slammed into the Siphon.

When the metal in his armor came into contact with the wires in the grid, countless volts of electricity started coursing through the Siphon's body. He was knocked off the stage and into a giant glass Planet Hollywood globe. Everything exploded in an amazing display of colored glass and sparking electricity.

"Best convention ever," one of the observers shouted to his friend.

Meanwhile, Jack hurried Seth and Sara down the escalator and into the casino, where he noticed a group of black-suited government agents ahead of him. He turned the kids in a different direction and started snaking through a maze of slot machines. But there were agents in every direction! In the middle of the group was Burke, smiling triumphantly as he moved toward them.

Jack frantically looked for an escape route. Suddenly an idea came to him.

He turned to Sara. "You listening to what I'm thinking?"

Sara smiled and nodded, message received. She focused her concentration, and after a moment, all the slot machines in the huge casino hit the jackpot. Hundreds of bells and sirens went off. Lights flashed wildly. Money started pouring out of the machines.

A riot erupted as gamblers deliriously scooped up piles of money. In the pandemonium, Burke lost sight of Jack and the siblings.

In the lobby, Alex stepped off the elevator, totally unaware of what had been happening. She heard all the noise and turned to see the casino in chaos. From the middle of it all, Jack and the kids came sprinting toward her at full speed. Grabbing Alex by the arm, he pulled her along with them.

"What happened to laying low?" she asked, running to keep up with them.

"Who lays low in Vegas?" Jack asked rhetorically. "Let's go!"

They hurried out of the casino.

By the time Burke and his men made it to the parking lot, they had no idea which way Jack and the others had headed. Burke was fuming.

As they raced to their SUVs, Burke saw something that changed his mood. It was Jack's cab swerving through the traffic, chased by the Las Vegas police.

Within seconds, Burke's SUV joined the pursuit and was quickly followed by the other SUVs.

The taxi jumped a curb and raced down an alley. As it hurtled toward the other end, the cab ricocheted off garbage cans and Dumpsters, tossing trash everywhere.

Just as the cab was about to make it out of the alley, another pair of SUVs arrived and blocked their escape. The taxi slammed on the brakes and came to a screeching halt.

Once the cars had all stopped, police officers leaped out, weapons drawn.

"We got them!" Burke announced, taking charge of the situation. He held up his arms and waved off the police as he approached the back of the taxi.

"*Our* suspects!" he ordered.

The door to the taxi opened, and for a moment, nothing happened. Then, three figures slowly stepped out into the alleyway.

Now Burke was raging mad.

There was no Jack, Seth, or Sara. It was Dr. Harlan and his two assistants.

Harlan smiled at the assembled group and gave Burke a wink.

"Greetings, Earthlings!"

CHAPTER 15

While Burke was busy with Harlan, Jack was driving Harlan's Winnebago toward California.

From the passenger seat, Alex looked over her shoulder at Seth and Sara sleeping in the back, totally exhausted by their adventure. Even in his sleep, Seth clutched the experiment tightly. Sara was snuggled up with Junkyard. "They survived a crash, are chased by our military, hunted by an assassin, and have the weight of two planets' survival on their shoulders," Alex said. "Unbelievable."

Jack took a glance at them in the rearview mirror and smiled. "They're lucky you joined us," he said. "*We're* lucky."

Alex laughed. "Luck had nothing to do with it. It's pure science," she claimed. "Chaos theory. The underlying order in apparently random data."

"So, more like . . . fate?" Jack observed.

"Science," she corrected. "Think about it. What are the odds that they would crash near Vegas during a UFO convention? *I* got in *your* cab. *They* got in *your* cab. And, now we're all in Harlan's mobile home loaded with *his* intel on where *their* ship is. That's not luck. That's a predetermined order of how things work in the universe."

Jack laughed. "So I was always going to meet you?"

"In theory," she said, a teasing note in her voice.

"And we were always going to help the kids get their spaceship out of the fortress?" he continued.

Alex nodded. "Science supports that logic."

For a moment they shared a look that was sweet and a bit awkward. They came from very different worlds, but an amazing chain of events—whether luck or chaos theory—had brought them together.

Hours later, they were within a few miles of Witch Mountain. Jack pulled the Winnebago off onto the side of the road.

"This is how it's going to go down," he explained. "You three will stay here. I go check out the mountain. If I can find a way in, I take it and look for your ship. If I can't, I come back and we take off. Understand?"

"Negative," Seth protested. "Sara and I will be going with you. It is our mission. It is our ship."

"Hold on," Alex interrupted. "I'm the one with all the maps. So, I'm not staying back here alone."

Sara looked Jack in the eye, once again reading his mind. She smiled. "It's okay, Jack Bruno," Sara said. "I know you are worried for our safety."

"If you can read my mind, then you already know—we can't win," he said.

Sara nodded. "But we can try. If not, our parents will be dead."

Jack took a deep breath. This was news to him.

"Without proof of their results," Sara explained, "they were sentenced to death."

"We have very little time left to get back home before our parents are executed," Seth added.

Jack and Alex exchanged looks.

"The fate of our parents and our two worlds are locked away inside Witch Mountain. Please, Jack Bruno, help us," Sara pleaded.

Jack looked at Alex. "Chaos theory, huh?"

CHAPTER 16

The terrain surrounding Witch Mountain made it difficult enough to reach, and the security made it practically impossible to enter.

They had to climb over rocky crags and through a fast-moving stream while evading surveillance cameras and a high-voltage fence.

Much to Jack's amazement, they made it all the way to a bluff overlooking the entrance—a giant archway carved right into a granite cliff. Military vehicles passed in and out through the heavily guarded entrance. It looked like there was no way the four of them could go through it.

"That's depressing," Alex said, looking over the situation. "Now what?"

Jack tried to think of something. "I was hoping chaos theory would deliver us a big tank or a battleship," he said. "Okay, new plan. We abandon the old plan."

Sara looked at him glumly. "You don't have a plan, do you?"

"I thought you could read minds," Jack said.

"I can," Sara said with a shrug. "I was just hoping I was wrong."

Alex pulled out one of the schematics from her backpack. "According to Harlan's intel there are several service tunnels spreading outward. Might be worth looking for."

Jack considered this for a moment. It was certainly better than trying to bust through the heavily guarded entrance. "That's what we call Plan B," he said. "Let's go."

But just as they started off, Sara began to wobble.

"Jack," she called out to him.

He rushed forward to keep her from falling. Her eyes were rolling backward and her eyelids were fluttering.

"What's wrong?" Alex asked, coming up beside Jack.

Jack grabbed hold of Sara, and when he did, she turned to the side, revealing the plastic tip of a dart sticking out of her neck.

Alarmed, Jack spun around. "Seth!" he called out. But it was too late.

Seth grabbed at his neck as he, too, started to stagger. Jack laid Sara down and rushed over to catch Seth before *he* fell.

Suddenly, twenty special operations soldiers emerged from the surrounding woods, as if by magic. Their camouflage had been perfect. Seconds earlier, they had blended in perfectly with the foliage. Burke led the team, a triumphant smile on his face. His mission had finally been accomplished.

"What did you do to them?" Alex demanded, her face ashen.

Burke gave her a disdainful look. "Consider yourself lucky. I could have you both shot on sight for trespassing and violation of U.S. government property."

Several soldiers approached carrying stretchers to take Seth and Sara away. Jack lunged to protect them, but another soldier took him out with two quick blows from the butt of his rifle. He fell to the ground. Jack tried to get up, but he was quickly knocked down again.

"Mr. Bruno," Burke said unsympathetically. "I have to believe that you're smart enough to know you can't win."

Jack looked over and watched as Seth and Sara were carried away. Even though they weren't fully conscious, their eyes pleaded with him to help.

There was nothing Jack could do but watch as the two were loaded into a Humvee.

"You have to listen to me," Alex pleaded. "It's absolutely vital that they get home!"

"They are home, Dr. Friedman," Burke said smugly. "They're now in my custody."

"You can't silence the truth," she warned him. "The world has a right to know of their existence."

"You're going to be the one to blow the whistle?" Burke asked with a laugh. "A failed astrophysicist, fired by three universities for obsessing over UFOs, teams up with a lifelong ex-con in declaring that the government has captured two normal-looking kids and is holding them hostage inside a mountain that doesn't exist? It's so much easier to let you speak than to deal with all the paperwork involved with killing you," Burke finished.

"Someone will believe us," Jack said.

"From behind bars?" Burke asked. "Let me remind you, Mr. Bruno, as a convicted felon, you're looking at twenty years just for standing on this mountain. Shall I go on?"

Jack turned to look at Alex, totally ashamed of what Burke had revealed—and what he was about to say.

"No," Jack assured him. "I get the message."

Burke eyed him for a moment, content that he had solved this problem for good. "Smart man," he said. "We'll give you a lift down. So much easier than walking up."

Alex turned to give Jack a searching look. "Wait," she pleaded. "That's it. It's over?"

"I'm sorry," he said, watching as disappointment flooded Alex's face.

They were quietly loaded into a Humvee and escorted back down the mountain with a driver and armed guard.

"Thankfully, Sara and Seth didn't have to witness how quickly you gave up," Alex fumed, her arms crossed in front of her. "They trusted you. *I* trusted you."

Jack had done what he could. Hadn't he told them he wasn't up for the job? "Well, join the club of everyone else in my life I've disappointed," he snapped.

The driver and guard shared a look as they listened in on the growing argument. The two in the back sounded like an old married couple.

"He'll dissect them like frogs in a high school biology class," she told him. "You know that."

"Whatever," Jack answered. "Not my problem."

That was it. Alex reached over and slapped Jack across the face.

The guard turned around to look. As he did, Jack timed a perfect punch to the jaw, knocking him out cold.

Before the driver could figure out what was happening, Jack lunged toward the front seat and forced the man's head into the window, shattering the glass in the process.

The driver lost consciousness, and the Humvee careened out of control. Jack quickly yanked the unconscious driver over the seat into the back, while Alex dived into the front and quickly grabbed the steering wheel. She managed to get control of the vehicle right before they would have slammed into a tree.

Once they came to a rest, Jack and Alex took deep breaths. Both driver and guard were out cold.

"When did you know?" Jack asked her, wondering how long it had taken her to figure out that he never intended to just give up.

"The minute they took your kids from you," she said with a knowing smile.

"The slap," he said as he rubbed his sore cheek. "Very realistic by the way."

"I'm very detail-oriented," Alex said with a laugh.

CHAPTER 17

Using one of Harlan's old maps, Jack and Alex were able to find the entrance to an abandoned service tunnel hidden beneath some scrub brush. They moved forward on their hands and knees until their way was blocked by a grate. Jack grunted and strained trying to push it open, but he couldn't budge it.

"For the record," Alex said, "I get very claustrophobic in tight places."

"*Perfect*," Jack thought as he maneuvered his body

around so that he could give the grate a couple of quick kicks. On the third try it finally popped off and fell down and out of sight. Jack kept waiting for the sound of the metal clanging against something, but there was no sound at all. The grate just kept falling. Jack took a deep breath before he looked over the edge and down into what appeared to be a bottomless pit.

"How are you with heights?" he asked, trying to force a smile.

The drop was at least two thousand feet. Jack was able to dangle over the edge and get his feet onto the rungs of a service ladder that was attached to the wall.

He signaled for Alex to follow. Slowly and very carefully she inched her way onto the ladder. Everything was okay until she looked down. Then she froze, too scared to speak or move.

"It's okay," Jack told her. "I am right below you."

"I . . . can't . . ." she stuttered. "You have to go without me."

"No way," Jack insisted. "I'm on this ladder.

You're on this ladder. This ladder leads us to Sara and Seth. Chaos theory, right?"

Alex gulped. "No theory," she said. "Just a lot of chaos." Still, his tone reassured her. Feeling a bit safer, she began to move.

As they climbed down, they discovered service tunnels every hundred feet or so. Jack wasn't sure which one he was looking for, but he hoped he would know it when he saw it.

Just then there was a loud and ominous grumble from deep below them.

"Earthquake?" Jack asked.

"Doubt it," said Alex. "The mountain was picked for its lack of seismic activity." At least, that was what Harlan's documents had said.

There was another, larger rumble that made the ladder shake. They had to hang on for dear life until Alex suddenly remembered something from one of the schematics.

"Oh, no, Jack," she yelled. "We've got to get out of here."

Jack looked down and saw a fiery red glow

coming up toward them.

"Exhaust furnace!" she shouted.

They hurried down to the next service tunnel as the fire rose. Jack ripped the grate off the entrance, and in one quick move he grabbed Alex and swung them both into the tunnel—just as the fireball shot past. The force of the explosion knocked them farther into the tunnel, which was slanted downward like a gigantic playground slide.

The two slid and tumbled until finally, Jack slammed into the bottom of the tunnel with a painful *thud*. A few seconds later, Alex landed on top of him.

When they crawled out of the tunnel, they were amazed by what they saw.

They were in the heart of Witch Mountain.

CHAPTER 18

Henry Burke sat in an all-white observation room that overlooked a high-tech laboratory. Seth and Sara were unconscious and connected to a series of wires and tubes in the lab. They were being examined by Matheson and Pope, each dressed in full medical gear.

"How soon until the subjects are prepped?" Burke asked, speaking into a microphone.

"They're heavily sedated," Matheson answered. "Minimal med tests proceeding within forty-eight to seventy-two hours."

Burke couldn't wait. "Unacceptable. Commence the procedures."

"We don't know enough about their systems," Matheson reminded him. "Any sudden change could terminate the subjects."

"You can't just kill them," Pope interjected.

"Mr. Pope, you'd do well not to forget what our mission is," Burke said. "Our orders come from Washington. And Washington wants answers."

Pope knew that it was useless to argue. He just nodded.

"Very good, then," Burke said. "Commence the tests."

Before they could begin, there was an eruption of sirens and alarms. From outside came the sounds of an explosion.

A panicked voice called in over the intercom. "We have penetration at fence sector twenty-eight!"

Something very bad was happening.

Burke and his team rushed out of the laboratory to find soldiers armed and charging toward the entrance of the mountain.

Burke looked at a monitor that showed a video of the outside. His eyes opened wide when he saw the enemy. The thing attacking his men was unlike anything he'd ever seen.

It was the Siphon.

As the battle raged near the mountain's entrance, Jack and Alex were able to slip into the laboratory unnoticed. Well, relatively unnoticed. They had to get by a few lab technicians first. With a few well-aimed punches, they got past the workers and put on new outfits. Wearing bio-suits, they rushed into the lab where Seth and Sara were being held.

"Come on," Jack pleaded as he tried to loosen their shackles. "Wake up!"

Alex read the label on the tank that fed into the tubes running to Seth and Sara. "It's some kind of anesthetic," she said. She quickly unscrewed the tubes from the tank and attached them to an oxygen supply.

The oxygen started to revive Seth and Sara. Suddenly Sara's shackles popped open. Jack looked over and saw her waking up. He turned to Seth, who was still woozy but strong enough to phase his wrists and ankles through his shackles.

"Jack, you came back for us!" Sara exclaimed.

Jack didn't speak. He just gave them both a big hug.

Now that they were free, they needed to find their ship. The compass and their parents' experiment were sitting on a nearby examination table. They each grabbed one and Seth turned on the homing mechanism in the compass.

"It's this way," Seth said, pointing to a nearby exit. They rushed out of the lab and down the hallway until they reached a giant hangar. Inside was their ship.

"We have to hurry," Sara told them.

"Tell *them* that," Jack said, pointing at the dozens of engineers who were working on the ship. "Maybe they'll just let us walk on out of here with it."

Alex thought about that for a moment and smiled. "Good idea."

Jack had no idea what she meant, but before he

could stop her, she grabbed a lab coat and put it on. Then she walked straight into the hangar.

"Excuse me?!" she exclaimed when she reached the group of engineers. "Do you not hear the alarms?"

The engineers looked back and forth among one another, confused.

"All work in this sector is to cease immediately," Alex continued. "We've got off-the-charts readings of sodium hypochlorite, xenon, hydrazine, and you don't want to know how bad the gamma radiation is."

"Who are you?" asked one of the engineers.

"Your worst nightmare at a court martial," Alex answered. "Now you can do as you're told, or I can go tell Henry Burke you disobeyed his direct orders!"

The mention of Burke's name did the trick. The engineers raced out of the hangar. Once they were gone, Jack, Seth, and Sara came to stand beside her.

"I can't believe that actually worked," Jack said with a laugh.

"Me neither," Alex answered.

Seth and Sara examined the spaceship. It had been damaged during their crash landing. Using her telekinesis, Sara made the ship fix itself. Alex watched in stunned amazement while Jack kept an eye on the door in case anyone returned.

It only took a few minutes to get the ship fully repaired. Once it was ready, the air-lock door slid open so they could all get on. They were almost in the clear. . . .

"Thank you," a voice called out from above. "We were having a hard time figuring that part out."

They looked up to see Burke on the upper level. Even with the battle raging outside, he was flanked by a group of soldiers, each with his gun aimed at them.

Jack instinctively moved forward and stood directly in front of the others.

"A brave but empty gesture, Mr. Bruno," Burke said.

"They're just kids," Jack called to him.

As they looked up at the soldiers, Seth grabbed Alex and Jack by the hand and Sara grabbed Jack's other hand. The four of them stood there defiant and united. Burke couldn't help but think they looked like a family.

Just then, an explosion caused by the approaching Siphon rocked the hangar. In the confusion, the soldiers began to fire at the foursome. But the bullets phased right through them. Seth had transferred his powers through their chain of hands.

Burke and the soldiers were stunned. They couldn't figure out what was happening.

But they didn't have time to try. There was another explosion, and one of the hangar walls erupted into fire. They all watched as the Siphon stepped through the flames.

The soldiers instantly turned their guns toward the Siphon.

"Go! Go! Go!" Jack shouted to the others, using the assassin's arrival to their advantage. They rushed up to the entrance and through the air lock.

"Stop them!" Burke yelled. "All of them!"

Now the soldiers were firing in every direction, some at the Siphon and others at the ship.

"We've got to get this thing up in the air!" Jack exclaimed once they were all safely on board. Seth and Sara grabbed the controls. The air lock hissed shut, thrusters fired up, and the ship slowly came to life.

"How do we get out of here?" Sara asked when the ship was floating.

"There!" Jack answered, pointing toward the gaping hole the Siphon had just made in the hangar wall.

Seth and Sara pointed the spaceship toward the hole. But standing in their way was the Siphon, determined to complete his mission. He raised his weapon and began firing right at the ship. Seth and Sara shared a quick look and then flew the space-craft right into the Siphon—and through the hole to safety.

CHAPTER 19

The spaceship shot high into the night sky and clear of Witch Mountain. Inside the cockpit, the four started cheering. Jack and Alex exchanged high fives while the kids manned the controls.

"You did it," Jack proudly exclaimed.

"*We* did it," Sara corrected.

But then the ship jolted from side to side. Seth looked down at the control panel.

"Air lock's jammed," he said. "I need to . . ."

Jack didn't let him finish. Seth needed to fly the

ship. He could take care of the air lock. Climbing down into the lower level, he heard the hiss of the open air lock. Jack shut it and turned to go, but just then an arm reached out and grabbed him by the throat. In the reflection of the shiny metal door he could see the Siphon's face.

Jack broke free and the two fell to the floor. He saw that the Siphon's weapon arm had been completely destroyed. His other arm, though, was ready to fight. The Siphon slammed into Jack, and the two started to trade punches, jolting the spaceship as they did.

Up in the cockpit, Seth turned to Alex. Jack was taking too long. Something must be wrong. "It takes two to pilot the ship," he told her. "You take the controls."

"What?" she exclaimed.

There was no time to argue. Seth bolted, and Alex nervously took his seat.

"I'm sure it's like flying a plane," Sara offered, trying to sound encouraging.

"Yeah," Alex shot back. "I don't do that, either."

Down below, Jack was barely holding his own against the Siphon when Seth arrived.

"Hey!" Seth yelled, distracting the assassin.

The Siphon turned to Seth. With one of his targets in sight, he ignored Jack and started to attack Seth. He threw a powerful punch, but it phased right through the boy.

This bought Jack just enough time to jump on the Siphon from behind. He grabbed him in a choke hold and pulled with all his might, yanking the Siphon's helmet off and revealing a hideously scary head.

"No wonder you're so angry," Jack said, moving away from the ugly creature.

The Siphon charged him, but Jack dodged the punches. With no helmet in the way, he was able to land a couple of punches directly on the Siphon's head.

Knocking the assassin to the floor, Jack accidentally opened the air-lock door. The sudden change in pressure caused the ship to lurch.

The Siphon tried to lunge at Seth, but Jack

whacked him across the face with the assassin's own helmet. The movement caused him and the Siphon to fly out the door. Jack clung to the edge of the ship, while the Siphon clutched Jack. If they fell, it would be into the ship's propulsion vortex and they would be killed instantly.

Jack held on to the ship with all of his strength and smiled.

"This ride's on me!" he said as he succeeded in knocking the Siphon loose. With an unearthly cry, the assassin fell directly into the swirling vortex. They were safe.

Standing on the ground next to the spaceship, Seth and Sara said their good-byes to Jack and Alex.

"Thankfully, the ship has only suffered minor damage," Seth explained. "We should be able to lock onto our planet's coordinates and return safely."

Seth and Sara exchanged a look. When she read his mind she smiled and gave him a nod.

"Sara and I want you to have this," Seth said.

Seth reached into his pocket and pulled out his

prized compass and handed it to Jack. Jack took a deep breath.

"As long as it is in your possession," Sara explained. "We will always be able to find you."

"Thanks," Jack said, choking up despite his best efforts.

"I want to apologize to you, Jack Bruno," Seth added. "I once said we could never count on humans to help us. Especially you. I was wrong."

Jack went to offer him his hand and thought better of it. He pulled him in for a hug. "You take care of yourself and your sister for me," Jack instructed him. "Understand."

"Yes," Seth answered. "This I completely understand."

Then it was Sara's turn. She asked them to take care of Junkyard—and each other. Jack started to say something. But Sara was able to read his mind and said it for him.

"I know," she answered. "We love you, too."

EPILOGUE

One year later, Jack and Alex returned to the UFO convention, only this time *they* were the stars. A packed audience hung on their every word as they finished their lecture.

They were talking about their best-selling book *Race to Witch Mountain: A True Story*. Pictures on the wall highlighted the amazing year they had just gone through. There were pictures of magazine covers, talk-show interviews, and international lectures, all featuring Jack and Alex.

"This information should not be in the hands of a secret cabal of men working deep within the dark corridors of the government," Alex said, wrapping up her speech. "But should be accessible to the public who have a right to know."

The audience erupted into cheers and applause. Jack and Alex shared a smile and waded through the crowd to the exit. Along the way they posed for pictures and autographed copies of their book.

Finally, as they waited for the valet to bring their car, another hand reached up with a copy of the book to be signed.

"Who do I make it out to?" Jack asked.

"Henry Burke," said the voice.

Jack and Alex both looked up, surprised to see the smiling face of their former enemy.

"Interesting read," Burke continued. "I especially liked chapter twelve. Wonderfully descriptive."

"I'm glad you enjoyed it," Jack said confidently. "You're going to like the next book even better."

"I very much look forward to that," Burke said with an eerie smile. "I'll see you both real soon."

Just then the valet arrived with their car. No longer driving a taxi, Jack hopped in behind the wheel of his dream car, a vintage Ford Mustang.

Alex got into the passenger seat; Junkyard was close behind. Suddenly, beeping started coming from Alex's purse. It was the compass. The light was flashing. Seth and Sara were on their way for a visit.

Jack and Alex looked deep into each other's eyes and smiled. They knew what that meant—more adventure was yet to come. And if they had learned anything, it was that the adventure was sure to be out of this world!